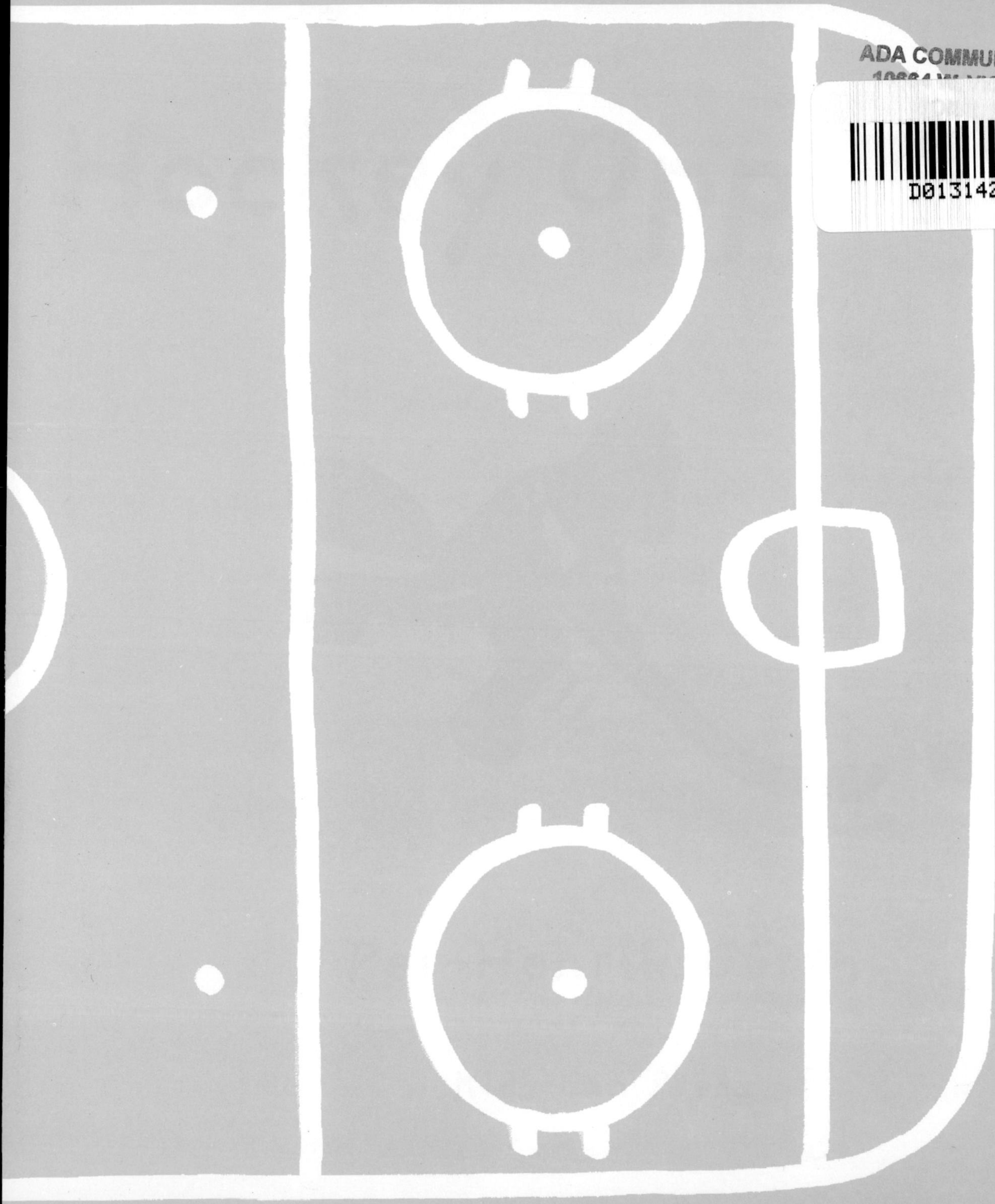

Home Team

Away Team

big

behind

ahead

out

in

smiles

frowns

one

many

down

miss

goal

loss

win

For Emily and Ben

Text © 2010 Kids Can Press
Illustrations © 2010 Per-Henrik Gürth

Kids Can Press acknowledges the financial support of the Government of
Ontario, through the Ontario Media Development Corporation's Ontario Book
Initiative; the Ontario Arts Council; the Canada Council for the Arts; and the
Government of Canada, through the BPIDP, for our publishing activity.

Published in Canada by
Kids Can Press Ltd.
29 Birch Avenue
Toronto, ON M4V 1E2

Published in the U.S. by
Kids Can Press Ltd.
2250 Military Road
Tonawanda, NY 14150

www.kidscanpress.com

The artwork in this book was created in Adobe Illustrator.
The text is set in Providence-Sans Bold and Good Dog Plain.

Written and edited by Yvette Ghione
Designed by Julia Naimska and Andrea Chomyn

This book is smyth sewn casebound.
Manufactured in Buji, Shenzhen, China, in 3/2010 by WKT Company

CM 10 0 9 8 7 6 5 4 3 2 1

Library and Archives Canada Cataloguing in Publication

Gürth, Per-Henrik
      Hockey opposites / written by Yvette Ghione ; illustrated by Per-Henrik
Gürth.
For ages 2 to 6.

ISBN 978-1-55453-241-4 (bound)

1. Hockey — Juvenile literature. 2. Polarity — Juvenile literature.
I. Gürth, Per-Henrik II. Title.

GV847.25.G52 2010   j796.962   C2009-906484-7

Kids Can Press is a l'orus™ Entertainment company

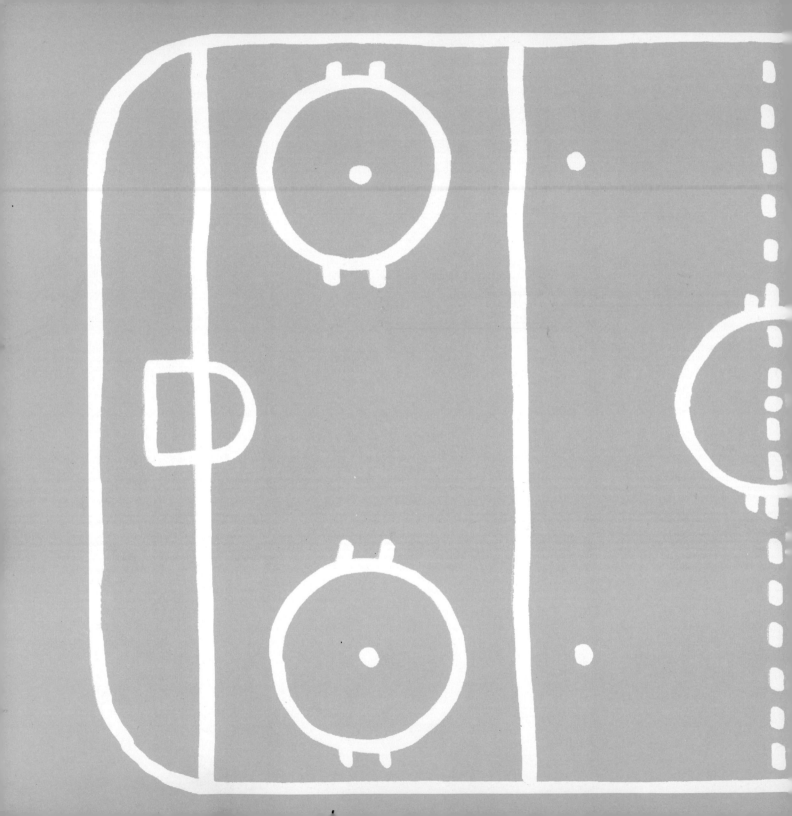